I TRIED CALLING

Written by Austin Abbott

Edited and Saved by Christian Craig

I TRIED CALLING by Austin Abbott

Independently published in 2023 by Austin Abbott
& Numerochair Films

All Rights Reserved. No part of this publication may be reproduced, distributed, or transmitted in any form or by any meams, including photocopying, recording, or other electronic or mechanical methods, without the prior written permission of the publisher, except in the case of brief quotations embodied in critical reviews and certain other noncommercial uses permitted by copyright law. For permission requests, write to the author at: austineabbott@gmail.com

This is a work of fiction. Names, characters, places, and incidents either are the product of the author's imagination or are used fictitiously.

Book designed by Austin Abbott

Cover photograph used with permission:
Jarrell, V. & Eiler, L. S. (1996) Vicky Jarrell prepares string beans while talking on the phone and sitting in a lounge chair in the living room. , 1996. [Photograph] Retrieved from the Library of Congress, https://www.loc.gov/item/cmns000610/.

Back cover photograph by Austin Abbott

Printed by Mixam

FIRST EDITION

ISBN: 979-8-218-24358-6

For Diana

1.
9:50 P.M., TUESDAY, AUGUST 12, 2014

MACHINE: One new message from Tuesday, August 12, 9:50 P.M.

[BEEP]

CHARLES: Hey, Alex, it's your pop. It's, uh, right near seven o'clock my time on Tuesday, let me see here, August 12th. So I guess that makes it, shit, around ten o'clock your time. Sorry about that. I'm sure you're tuckin' the girls in now. Or... maybe you, do you do that earlier? Hell, you always wanted to stay up late, so I don't know what time the kiddos are 'sposed to be goin' to bed.

[SIGH]

CHARLES: I was on the Facebook and saw your Aunt Marsha put on her page a news story that Robin Williams died. I went to send it to you but I can't find your Facebook site. Did you erase it? Anyway, I saw it happened yesterday, so maybe you already knew. Just awful. Such a funny man.

[PROLONGED EXHALE]

CHARLES: Hope you're not too sad about it, I know how much you loved the guy. As much as you can love somebody you don't know, anyway. I remember when I took you to see the nanny one he did, where he dresses up like that old lady. You got such a kick out of him with them fake tits, you were laughin' your little ass off. You had to be, what, ten years old? Aw man, I remember that weekend like it was yesterday. Or most of it, anyway. Your Uncle Danny was around, and you know what we were gettin' into back then. Though you were probably asleep for all that. At least I hope so, shit!

[LAUGHING. COUGHING.]

That Sunday you wanted to go to church, but I figured that was just your Mama talkin', so I said HELL no. You bitched a little bit. You weren't always like that, but man, when you got like that you were an annoying little shit. I threw you in the pickup anyway. Had the '82 Chevy Silverado then, loved that thing, the only bitch that never let me down!

[LAUGHING. COUGHING. A CAN OPENS.]

CHARLES: Anyway, we, uh, we drove up to Bakersfield for this little dirt bike show your Uncle Danny was putting on, and you were still pitchin' a fit, actin' like you didn't like it, but when Jackie Reynolds damn near broke his fuckin' neck, you were laughin' as hard as you were at them fake titties!

Your Mama got pissed 'cause I didn't let her know I was running a day or two late on gettin' you back home, but when she called me that week, yellin' into the phone 'bout how you were askin' for a dirt bike, I lost it! It was all worth it then. Shit. We musta seen some other Robin Williams movies after that too. The one with the board game with the animals? You didn't care about that one much. I only took you on account of how much you loved the nanny one. You were mad at me 'cause I hadn't been around much, but that was all your Mama. Blame me all you want, and God rest her soul, but she could really be the bitch of the ball when she wanted to be.

[SIPPING]

CHARLES: I'm sure you're sad today. I tried to tell you yesterday but I couldn't find your Facebook website. Your Uncle Danny ain't doin' so great now. Liver cancer. Thought it went away last year but I guess the doctors were wrong. Say a prayer if you're still doin' that. How are the girls gettin' on? When are you gonna take 'em out west to meet their Papa? We could all watch that nanny movie, maybe they'd have a good laugh, too. Maybe you can...

[COUGHING. SIPPING.]

CHARLES: Maybe you can come out here for Christmas? I know Lauren's got a stick up her ass about me. No offense to you, I'm sure she's great with the girls.

I'm seein' a nice lady. Maureen. She's no Farrah Fawcett but she's funny enough and makes damn good pork chops. She made me go try sushi! Imagine that, your old man eatin' that Asian fish. Well, I'll let you go. Just wanted to let you know about Robin Williams. Tell Lauren 'bout Christmas, I'm—I'm a better man now. The last time you saw me, I was... I shouldnt'a brought that shit to your wedding. Barely doin' shit besides some beer these days. Just wanna meet the girls and see you. Alright.

[PHONE CLICKS]

2.
5:45 P.M., WEDNESDAY, AUGUST 12, 2015

MACHINE: One new message from Wednesday August 12, 5:45 P.M.

[BEEP]

JESSICA: Hi, Kerry, It's Jessica! I just wanted to go over a few things before Small Group tomorrow night. You had mentioned that you've never led one before. So exciting. You don't need to be nervous at all, it's a breeze, and the group is super receptive and open. Andreas and Kelly said that they would lead worship—I don't think you've heard Andreas sing? He actually made it past the first round on The Voice! He didn't make the TV part, but it was still super exciting.

So you'll lead in prayer and the actual study itself. We sent you the notes in an email, but let me know if you need it again—Oh! And then the icebreakers! Those are always my favorite part. I like to get a little funky with mine. Well, I mean, you've seen some of the ones I've done before… But, like, "Who's singing voice would you take if you could?" or, like, "What was your favorite cartoon as a kid?" For those, mine would be Carrie Underwood and VeggieTales. I know that sounds like cheating—to give a Christian answer—but my Dad didn't want us watching TV as a kid, so we really only got cartoons in Sunday School. Plus, it's nice to have answers that can bring the focus back to the real point of the group. That's a helpful tip, maybe!

The only thing I'd say up front is that we try to veer away from, like, politics. And political stuff. I saw on your Facebook that you're very passionate about some things, which is awesome! You're such an eloquent writer, but for Small Group, we just want to direct that passion more toward the Lord and less toward the law. Personally, I have no problem with it, but some of the people who come have parents in law enforcement, or are even in law enforcement themselves. Do you know Brian? With the red hair? He's actually a police officer in Newburgh! Imagine the stress he feels during work, and then to have to come to a bible study just to be caught off guard by the wrong sentiment...

So obviously, we want to make sure everyone feels welcome. I'm sure if you came one week and the message was about, like, I don't know like, well, I don't want to say anything offensive, but you know what I mean? You get it, right? Honestly, nothing to be stressed about! The group loves you and your awesome and unique point of view. Most people here haven't really traveled much, so it's fun to have an out-of-towner. Well, actually, I guess a bunch of us did go to West Virginia for a mission trip and—wait, you're from there, right? Or was it regular Virginia? West Virginia was so sad, but like, awesome. The group has wanted to organize another trip soon, maybe we can talk about that tomorrow. Do you know any places where you're from that need to be helped? I've suggested we stay local, but it's more fun for people to go away from home to serve. Plus, with everything so sensitive... Like, I'm not sure if someone like Brian would want to do a food drive in one of the neighborhoods he patrols, and then there are some other concerns...

So anyway, for the game afterwards, some people will be continuing Settlers of Catan from last week, but we should probably think of another game for the rest of the group. Apples to Apples is always fun. But I'll leave that up to you! I'll bring a few just in case, though. So I guess that's it for now, if you have any questions for me just call. Ah! And I'm bringing brownies! Can't wait to hear your message, praying for you, girl!

[PHONE CLICKS]

3.
11:45 A.M., TUESDAY, FEBRUARY 2, 2021

VOICEMAIL: One new message from Tuesday, February 2, 11:45 A.M.

[BEEP]

[MUFFLED SOUNDS]

ANGELICA: last, so give us a call at your earliest convenience— Hello, this is Angelica, with the financial relief center. I'm reaching out to inform you about a recent lawsuit settlement that now requires the IRS to settle all outstanding tax debt any US resident currently carries. This means your tax debt can now be forced into a settlement on your behalf. Give us a call back and one of our agents can get you enrolled today. My number is 1-865-837-0374. Again, that's 1-865-837-0374. We aren't sure how long this will last, so give us a call at your earliest convenience.

Hello, this is Angelica with the finan—
[PHONE CLICKS]

4.
3:15 A.M., TUESDAY, AUGUST 20, 2019

MACHINE: One new message from Tuesday, August 20, 3:15 A.M.

[BEEP]

ALI: Hey.

[EXTENDED PAUSE]

ALI: It's me. I'm assuming you're asleep, or just didn't want to pick up, which makes sense, 'cause it's what? 2:30…

[MUFFLED NOISES]

ALI: … 3:13 A.M. You're probably asleep. I'm just leaving this message 'cause I called a bunch of times, and you're gonna see a bunch of missed calls, so—

[PAUSE]

The apartment burned down. Or, like, was on fire. I guess we don't know the total damage yet. But it's, like, fucked. Nancy, from next door? She knocked over a candle and didn't realize, or something. I'm fine, I guess I should say. I was alone. Of course. I mean—I was alone. I'm at my sister's place now. I guess I didn't really need to call, but, I don't know. I called. Fuck. I mean, you texted me when your fish died. I didn't know who to call. Also, I'm like, drunk, ish, now? But whatever. I called you.

[SIPPING]

ALI: You know how people ask what you'd grab in a fire? Like, as an icebreaker? I grabbed my laptop, and I grabbed Ralphie Bear, and then I looked around and I didn't know what else to grab. I should have, like, ran out right then, but…

I left the cassette you made me, the one where you added fake DJ lines between the songs. I left the painting of the clowns with the dogs from Prospect Park. It was still hanging up, but I left it.

I went to the kitchen, looked into the sink, and I know I should have just ran out, but… But I looked down into the sink and I saw that mug from that thrift store we found when we went upstate. I remember that you bought a Tom Petty CD but didn't realize you were wearing a Tom Petty shirt, so when you were ringing up you were all embarrassed and were like, "This is a coincidence," to the old lady who was working there and she was just like, "What?" and we had to run out 'cause we were cracking up—

[MUFFLED SOUNDS]

ALI: No, sorry, I'm—Okay. Okay, goodnight, Em.

[MUFFLED SOUNDS]

ALI: Sorry, I'm at Emily's. I told you that, I think. But anyway, after that we went to that little ceramic painting class I had the Groupon for. I was trying really, really hard. I could tell you didn't want to be there, even though you were really trying, too, which I think is what makes it even more fucking sad. It was like when you're on a first date with someone and you know it's not going anywhere, except you're already engaged. Whatever. But that mug we painted that day, when we were in the car back home, you said, "this is the first new mug we got since we've been together. All the others were inherited." Which I hated—that you said "inherited," it sounds so dramatic, even though I think it's the right word. So I saw this mug sitting in the sink and

I left that, too. Anyway, you don't have to call me back. But I needed to tell you how gone everything is.

[PHONE CLICKS]

5.
8:52 P.M., MONDAY, AUGUST 7, 2006

MACHINE: One new message from Monday, August 7, 8:52 P.M.

[BEEP]

RONALD: Hello, Pastor Rick, this is Ronald Haig. I'm sorry to be calling you this late in the night, and especially during your vacation week. The thing is, sir, well I'm in a bit of a predicament here. It's Monday the 7th, I believe around 9:00 P.M. I'm here at Grace. I'm—well, I'm in the basement and I can't get out right now. My keys are on the outside of the door, and I did not know that the basement door locks from the inside. Again, I'm so sorry to be calling now, I just don't have too many numbers in the cell phone here, and you had given me your personal number on the staff retreat to Cooperstown a few months back, so you're the best bet I've got. Melinda has told me that you and some of the other pastors on staff have a strict no-phone policy for after hours, so this, well, this does feel like a long shot, as I'm not sure whether that policy extends to your vacation time. Which, I should say, I hope you're enjoying! You and the family picked a beautiful week to get out of town. Send my regards to Elizabeth and Caleb and McKenzie. Maybe the kids don't know me, but I'm sure Elizabeth does. She makes sure to say hello to me on Sundays. A warm woman.

I should mention... Well, I've been debating on whether to say this or not, but I believe I may be under the influence of drugs at the moment, Pastor. I work at the store during the week, I believe I told you this, the sporting goods store over on 94— you mentioned Caleb has been playing hockey, please come in any time, I can help him get some good stuff for cheap. Anyway, my boss is a few years—I suppose many years—my junior, and Pastor, I've been having a real hard time with him. A coworker of mine, Chantal, she brought brownies to the store. She made it clear that they were not for me, but Travis, my manager, insisted I take some home. So, before I came here to clean for the night, I had one of the brownies. I called Chantal to tell her how delicious it was, and she sounded both alarmed and bemused that I had eaten one. That's when I became suspicious. Travis is always messing with me, Pastor. I don't like him and I'm struggling to not curse him. I think your sermon last week was very strong and powerful and I've really been thinking about "taming the tongue," as I do not want to curse man with the same tongue I use to praise the Lord. But I am struggling, Pastor.

[EXTENDED PAUSE]

RONALD: I don't do drugs, so I am scared now. I'm feeling a little funny and I am thinking it's not great that I am here in the basement. If you get this, please send someone to the church to let me out. As I'm sure you remember, the whole staff took off this week, so no one will be in tomorrow morning. I'm—

[EXTEND PAUSE]

RONALD: The nativity scene statues from the Christmas play are down here and they gave me a startle. Now Pastor, do you think that, and please correct me if I'm misreading this, but do you think that in James, when he says, "but no human being can tame the tongue. It is a restless evil, full of deadly poison," that he means we should get rid of the tongue? Like, really get rid of it? I know there have—I'm sorry, I'm feeling a bit lightheaded here—I know there are people who actually have cut the tongues straight out of their mouths. Do you think that's ever good? It sounds crazy, but I guess a lot of things that honor the Lord "sound" crazy until examined through the lens of the holy spirit. I don't—

[EXTENDED PAUSE]

RONALD: Hello? Is somewhere there? HELLO?

[PAUSE]

RONALD: Pastor Rick, this is Ronald Haig. Hope you are well. If you get this, please call another member of the church staff to come unlock this basement to—I just, I just saw the eyes of Joseph move. They just moved. Very slightly, but they moved. That's okay. Holy shit. Oh, Pastor, I'm so sorry, there's that wild tongue again. The untamable beast.

Pastor, I got to reading more of James 3 in one of the Bibles down here, and these verses came next: "But if you harbor bitter envy and selfish ambition in your hearts, do not boast about it or deny the truth. Such 'wisdom' does not come down from heaven but is earthly, unspiritual, demonic. For where you have envy and selfish ambition, there you find disorder and every evil practice." I am envious of my manager Travis. I don't like him and I want to be his leader, not he mine.

[SNIFFLING]

RONALD: I try to be a good man. don't want the Devil in me just because I want to be manager at Touchdown Thrifts. I will give up that selfish desire. Please pray for me, Pastor. I am praying that you break your rule about no phones after hours so you can help break me of these demonic chains and free me from this basement...

[SNIFFLING. THROAT-CLEARING.]

RONALD: Pastor Rick, this is Ronald Haig. Hope you are well. If you get this, please let Melinda or someone know that I am trapped in the basement of the church and may be under the influence of drugs. I hope you're enjoying your vacation and please give my regards to Elizabeth and the children.

[PHONE CLICKS]

6.
10:42 A.M., THURSDAY, MAY 13, 2004

VOICEMAIL: One new message from Thursday, May 13, 10:42 A.M.

[BEEP]

RYAN: Yo, just calling you back. Guess I'll have to wait until you call me back to miss your call and then do this over again. Excited to talk to you instead of your machine one day.

I was at Walmart last night. I got off work and didn't want to go home. I guess I needed a light bulb, but really I just felt like walking around. So I go to the section with all the posters, the rack with all of 'em on the carousel? I flip through and I see Jimi Hendrix, Carmen Electra, the ones you always see. And then I see that Albert Einstein one, with the tongue out and shit. Remember when Mom got us one of those that time we did Christmas at her house?

[LAUGHING]

RYAN: I was trying to remember why. We didn't even know who he was, Frank called us retarded when he found out. We hung it up for like a month until Dad figured out we didn't know who the fuckin' guy was and let us take it down.

But it just clicked for me: Mom was working at Walmart that year. She probably forgot to buy any presents and just grabbed whatever poster was still there on Christmas Eve. Amazing. I was very happy to make this connection. Twenty-six years later. Felt like you'd enjoy it, too. Okay, call me back.

[PHONE CLICKS]

7.
3:46 P.M., MONDAY, MAY 15, 2017

MACHINE: One new message from Monday, May 15, 3:46 P.M.

[BEEP]

CALLIE: Helen?! Pick up! I know you're home! Pick up pick up pickuppickup, bitch! Alex, if you're listening, it's your Aunt Callie, give the phone to Mommy! Okay, listen, I'll assume you're grabbing the mail or something and are coming back any minute now, so I'll just explain because I've already called your cell, like, ten times. I met someone at Radio Room the other night, and before you say anything—just don't. It's actually very normal to meet people out in the real world like this. You should be happy that I'm not relying on Tinder or Bumble or… Lesbian Farmers Only, or whatever.

Anyway, she's coming over for dinner tonight, and I'd planned to make this lemon chicken thing because I was feeling ambitious at the store. I got all the stuff for it last night and then I was looking at her Instagram this morning and remembered she's VEGAN, which, like, bleh, but whatever, and—SHIT! Dad's supposed to come over to fix my dishwasher tonight. Goddamnit. He's gonna want to stay for dinner. He's done that before, you know. When I first started dating Meghan, he showed up unannounced because he was "in the neighborhood," 'cause of course he just happens to be twenty-five minutes away from his house on a Tuesday right after work. But anyway, he came over halfway through dinner and ended up staying the whole night. They talked about Fleetwood Mac. Love to listen to Dad go on about Tusk instead of getting laid.

[EXHALE]

CALLIE: Anyway, I was going to order from that vegan place downtown, but I just saw they're closed on Mondays. Listen, I know this is my fault. Yes, I'm a big stupid bitch. But—I know John tried to be vegan for, like, ten minutes a few years ago, and you told me you made something you actually liked one time, so I need that recipe. If you don't call me back I'm going to go to McDonald's and get, like... fries? Wait, they make salads. That's not the worst idea, I can just throw it in a bowl. They probably, like, fry their lettuce in bacon grease or something, though—wait, is this you?

[MUFFLED NOISES]

CALLIE: It's just spam.

[MUFFLED NOISES]

CALLIE: Why would I ever suggest having dinner at my apartment? Why did I do that? I don't cook. I think it's because when I cooked those pork chops for you last month, you loved them, and John got seconds, and you said he never gets seconds. Imagine if I just made her pork chops? Is there anything less vegan-sounding than "pork chop?" A truly violent dish. Even pork sounds violent.

How have you not called me back yet? Are you dead? Now I'm getting concerned. I would hate to hear myself say "are you dead?" on your machine while we're like, cleaning out your house. What are you doing this weekend? Are you going to Mom's? Dad asked me to come over, probably because he thought we'd be going to Mom's. I hate when he does that, but also, I get it. Plus, Mom was so weird last time we came over. Now that she's "reclaiming her catholicism," or whatever the fuck. Wait! Are you calling me back now...

[MUFFLED NOISES]

CALLIE: Ugh, it's Dad. I have to call him. Listen, call me back or I'll never talk to you again! I truly hope that you are not, in fact, dead. Love you!

[PHONE CLICKS]

8.
11:45 P.M., THURSDAY, APRIL 28, 1994

MACHINE: One new message from Thursday, April 28, 11:45 P.M.

[TAPE CLICKS]

RENEE: Hey girl, it's Renee. Just wanted to call because... It's official! After ten years, I am no longer a bartender at Ralph's. It feels good! Weird, but good. I know you had that thing with Jared tonight, but I'm sad you weren't there. Alex and Frankie and Kyra came by. It was busy at first, 'cause of the Nuggets game, but the Sonics blew 'em out so it got quieter pretty quick. It was just fun. Reminiscing and talking shit. Ellen was goin' on about when you and Shawn spit in that one asshole's shot, and then he got so drunk he tripped and broke his nose on the pool table.

[LAUGHING]

RENEE: I'm gonna miss it. I didn't think I would, but I'm gonna. I'm glad we started talking again. That was so dumb, it's weird to even think about now. And look where we ended up! Now you're out with Jared, seven years later, and I'm moving away with Bill.

I'm going to miss the quiet days the most. Those days in the winter when there's no games on and the holidays are over and everything is just... I don't know. There was this guy that came in a lot, I don't know if you met him, you were working afternoons back then. But this guy, I think his name was Kent, he would do these—I mean, I don't know if he did it professionally or anything, but he would do these little magic tricks if it was quiet enough at the bar. I asked him why he did them one time, and he said he wanted to make sure someone in the world always thought magic was real. He was corny, but I liked him. Always got whiskey sours. He stopped coming in a few years ago. We would know these people for a few nights a week, they'd come in for years sometimes, and then one day they'd be gone and you'd never see them again. No one ever says goodbye. That's okay, we're more of a place to say hello. That's why it feels weird now. Kyra and Alex got me a trophy that says "Ralph's Worst Chugger," which cracked me up, but—

[MUFFLED NOISES]

RENEE: Well, I'm excited. I keep talking like I'm sad but I really am excited. This place sucks, you know? I'm excited to have healthcare. To not smell like barbecue when I get home at two in the morning. What's it like to smell like nothing? That sounds amazing. I won't even buy perfume anymore because I just want to smell like whatever the new office will smell like. Printer paper? Oh, and I'm not going to miss the asshole high school football coaches that would come in every week, grabbin' girls asses. Not gonna miss the seventeen-year-olds using fake IDs so they can stiff us on tips.

[SIGH]

RENEE: See, I'm sad and I'm happy! And, I don't know, maybe nervous, too. Maybe everyone at this new job will be an asshole. People think people who live in cities are assholes, but we both know a hell of a lot of assholes here, too. Now I'm just rambling. Sorry. When I took a shot with everyone and we all slammed the glasses down on the bar and I looked at the bottoms of all the empty shot glasses, it felt like a metaphor or something. You know what I mean? I think you probably do. I'm glad we had our time there, even if a lot of it was stupid. Well yeah, that's all.

[PHONE CLICKS. TAPE CLICKS.]

9.
9:17 A.M., MONDAY, SEPTEMBER 19, 2016

VOICEMAIL: One new message from Monday, September 19, 9:17 A.M.

[BEEP]

DOROTHEA: Good afternoon, Frances. This is Dorothea, at Rockland Fire and Safety. The telephone number here is 845-277-8152. I had called you a couple weeks ago because it looks like you are past due for our annual inspection! I'm sure I don't need to remind you that we were last out there on August 15th of 2015, so we wanted to make sure we get over there during the month of September. It's extremely important to the whole staff here that this happens in a timely and cordial manner—and this goes without saying, but we don't want to repeat our last visit's incident. I'll just leave it at that. So, when you get a chance, please give us a call at 845-277-8152. Once again, this is Dorothea, that's D-O-R-O-T-H-E-A, calling in regard to the fire inspection.

[PHONE CLICKS]

10.
5:18 P.M., SATURDAY, JUNE 25, 2006

MACHINE: One new message from Saturday, June 25, 5:18 P.M.

[BEEP]

SAM: Hello, Erin, this is Sam—and also Erin. Erin, say Hi to You in the Future.

ERIN: Hi, Me in the Future!

SAM: That was you from the past. We're calling to record some working ideas for the band name so we don't forget them. Erin, why are we doing this?

ERIN: Because you can lose a list, but you can't lose sound waves.

SAM: Yes. And because we're high. Okay, potential band name number one is...

ERIN: Xylophobic. Xylophobic rules because it's four syllables, like so many other great bands.

SAM: Very interesting. What other band names have four syllables?

ERIN: Mastodon.

SAM: That's three.

ERIN: Incubus.

SAM: Also three.

ERIN: System of a Down.

SAM: That's five.

[LAUGHING]

ERIN: Okay, shit. Uh… Alien Ant Farm.

SAM: Why don't we focus on another reason Xylophobic works.

ERIN: Okay, well, it's like xylophone, but also… phobic. Like you're afraid of a xylophone. Fear of Music. And xylo is such a good sound.

SAM: That's great. Potential band name number two: Jinglewood.

ERIN: This one is yours.

SAM: My dad is from Inglewood, and it's like… adding a jingle bell in front of it. Very straightforward word mash, like Xylophobic.

ERIN: My one con—if we're doing pros and cons—it's very Christmas-y.

SAM: Future Erin, would you like to comment?

ERIN: Imagine if I knew what I was going to say.

SAM: No input from Future Erin. Jinglewood is out. Okay, next up we've got what I think is a pretty good one: The Squid Accident.

ERIN: I'm neutral on this one.

SAM: It's sophisticated!

ERIN: I don't think the letter "Q" is in many sophisticated words.

SAM: What about... Queen? Quizzical?

ERIN: Queen is a good one. Point taken.

SAM: The Squid Incident is in play.

ERIN: I thought you said accident?

SAM: Did I? I wrote Incident here.

ERIN: Incident is better.

SAM: The Squid Accident is out. Squid Incident is in.

ERIN: We should probably learn how to play music, too.

SAM: Let's not go crazy, here.

ERIN: Did you see that? That squirrel just jumped over that bird?

SAM: Focus! Future Erin, don't mind Present Erin, she's high. Wait, is it Present Erin, or Past Erin?

ERIN: You focus! Next band name! This one is so good.

SAM: Get ready, Future Us.

ERIN: Okay, here it is: KELSER GRAMMY. Kelser. Grammy. It's so good!

SAM: Damn. Very good. Hearing it out loud... I don't think we can beat Kelser Grammy.

ERIN: God, it sounds so good. And it was organic, too! Just said it out loud while watching Frasier.

SAM: I think that's it. I mean we've got The Love Boat Shoes, Lubbock County Vampire Association—

ERIN: I still love that one.

SAM: Up in Smocks, Alabaster Legacy, XXYYZZAABBCC—

ERIN: That's the worst one. That one sucks.

SAM: I'm crossing that one out. Shouldn't have even made the list.

ERIN: I'm so hungry. What do you want to do for dinner?

SAM: Orlando's?

ERIN: Oh my god, the ravioli. We have to.

SAM: I am… very baked right now. Goddamn.

ERIN: Should we call Deb and Pat and ask if they want to come?

SAM: Come where?

ERIN: To Orlando's.

SAM: Ah yes. Raviolis. I don't know. We just saw them two days ago.

ERIN: Just call them! We can split the bill.

SAM: Where's my phone?

[MUFFLED NOISES]

SAM: Oh shit, we're still leaving you a message.

[LAUGHING]

ERIN: Oh my god, I forgot we were on the phone with me.

SAM: Okay, I'm hanging up now. Say bye to Future Erin.

SAM & ERIN: Bye Future Erin!

ERIN: Kelser Grammy Forever!

SAM: What's Pat's num—

[PHONE CLICKS]

11.
9:06 P.M., FRIDAY, DECEMBER 5, 2014

MACHINE: One new message from Friday, December 5, 9:06 P.M.

[BEEP]

JUSTIN: Hey man. This is Justin. Guess I don't really need to say that. I talked to Ben, they said they were going to turn your phone off this week. I was just at your wake.
It was weird. There were a few kids from our class there. Jack Reilly and Caitlin Peña came together, which was weird. I got to talk to Marcos, which was nice. Hadn't talked to him in years. I guess it's been a while since we talked, too. I mean, like, talked-talked.

They had the thing to kneel on to pray in front of your casket. So I did, because the person in front of me did. You looked good. You looked like you, which, I don't know, I feel like doesn't always happen. My Grandma didn't look like her. I wish I never looked at her casket. I'm glad I looked at yours. I couldn't pray, though. So I guess that's why I'm calling you, or your phone, now.

[LONG BREATH]

JUSTIN: We met in '98, right? In Mrs. Flanagan's class? I think you were the first person to talk to me after I'd moved there. You were the first person to invite me to a sleepover, too. I still remember it perfectly. We went to Blockbuster to pick a movie, and I wanted to get Tomorrow Never Dies, and you wanted to get the James Bond game, so we watched the movie and then played the video game. That blew my mind. I didn't have any video-game stuff at my house. I think that was the same night your brother nailed you in the eye with a TV remote. We stayed up late to watch South Park, which I definitely wasn't allowed to watch, so I rode that high for like a week. Then we got hungry and we wanted to make eggs, but didn't know how, so we stuck two eggs in the microwave for a few minutes, and of course they exploded, and—

[LAUGHING]

JUSTIN: —and your mom came down and called you a dumbass, which also was the first time I'd ever heard an adult cuss.

[SIPPING DRINK. SIGHING.]

JUSTIN: I saw her at the wake, your mom. I was going to say something, but then, I don't know, I didn't say anything. I wish we hung out more. You were always with Jake and Isaiah and that crew and I didn't really mesh with them. You would go to Ocean Beach with all those guys, and at first I wasn't allowed to go, but then I just wasn't invited, which is fine. I don't know. It just feels weird. You did seem really happy, which is good. A lot of people aren't happy. I'll try to see if there's anything I can do to help your family. There probably isn't. I mean, we worked at the same mall. I'm just, I don't know. This is stupid, and I probably shouldn't even be doing it in case anyone listens to these before they shut your line off. If anyone else is listening, just—whatever. I'm really glad that I knew you, man. I hope you're at peace. I'll miss you.

[PHONE CLICKS]

12.
2:11 P.M., TUESDAY, APRIL 30, 2002

VOICEMAIL: One new message from Tuesday, April 30, 2:11 P.M.

[BEEP]

RANDY: Helen, hi. This is Randy, I was the sax man in the band at your wedding last Friday. I got your number from the contract. How are you? I hope the honeymoon was as fun as could be. I love seeing the bride off to her honeymoon, I can always see that look in her eyes. Ravenous, ready for her knight in shining armor. Believe me, I should know. No instrument is more sensual than the sax.

You guys were great. Great wedding. I was just thinking about that conga line. Conga lines are really where someone in my position gets to shine, especially in the lead. So anyway, I'm calling for somewhat of a strange reason. Well, not strange to me, but I would imagine it might be strange to you.

[LAUGHING]

RANDY: Your maid of honor, Isabelle. Wow. Just drop-dead gorgeous. Don't get me wrong, she had nothing on the bride… But Isabelle's hips… Helen, I'm an honest man with no shame. I watched her dance while I was playing. I could tell she's a spirit of the wind, like me. Helen, I mean, I'm sure you've recognized her allure, you're her best friend. But enough gushing, I would love to shoot Isabelle. Not shoot her—capture her. Through photography, I mean.

[LAUGHING, COUGHING]

RANDY: I'm something of an amateur photographer when I'm not fingering the horn. My work is inspired by the art of the renaissance, a time in which I feel humans were operating a bit closer to our true nature. It was an era of rejuvenation, of discovery. Vulnerability. When I look at those paintings, or when I spend time at the faire, I see people with their guards DOWN. My photography, my art, it showcases the female form in the spirit of the renaissance, that rawness, that fertility. I would absolutely love it if you could connect me with Isabelle.

It'd be part of a specific series called The Excommunication of Flesh. A lot of it's positioned around the church of the time. I could send you, or her—both of you ladies—some of the images I've created so far. It's such a meaningful project, it really brings the value of God into question. And I say that with all due respect, I'm a spiritual person. And for all Excommunication levels against organized religion, it's ultimately a celebration of the female form. I know this probably sounds forward, but I always feel like I really know someone after playing their wedding. If the rhythms I provide can make your body move, then we're really connected in a way a lot of people just aren't. I mean—

[MUFFLED NOISES]

RANDY: I don't have a lot of published work, currently, with politics the way they are. You know how it is... I'm hoping to do a show in our basement. I share a home with Allen and Marjorie, the drummer and keyboard player from the band. We're looking to hang some of my pictures, and I really feel Isabelle could be the showcase image for this show.

So, if you could, I'd love it if you'd pass along my information. I put my card in her purse at the wedding with a little note. Haven't heard back yet, so I'm assuming she just hasn't seen it. You know how women's purses are! I've heard some funny jokes about that. Anyway, I don't want to keep you too long here. So again, congrats on the wedding. Blessings!

[PHONE CLICKS]

13.
11:35 A.M., FRIDAY, JULY 17, 1987

MACHINE: One new message from Friday, July 17, 11:35 A.M.

[TAPE CLICKS]

CINDY: Hey, Linda! Cindy Dwyer again. I called earlier about the audition for Family Ties... you probably haven't heard anything about that yet, right? I'm still home, so I would have gotten your call. BUT—I actually had this idea I wanted to run by you. I was watching PBS this morning and remembered you'd told me about a connection you had over at KVVT—someone you met at a dinner or something? But I was thinking we could pitch a children's show for an afternoon slot? That's a dead zone right now, and like, some kids are still home, you know? My sister, Angie, she started homeschooling my nephew, Travis, and she's done early, so he's just sitting there with nothing to do for a few hours until the kid's programs come back on or until the other kids get back from school. Or, like, sick kids? Or young kids? Linda, I feel like this could be huge! And I've got ideas. I could host, obviously, but like, as a character, and I was thinking... maybe a giraffe?

[SIPPING DRINK]

CINDY: We'd obviously have to check the rights. Like, to see if Toys 'R' Us owns the rights to giraffes? I think that'd be hard to do, honestly. To own the rights to giraffes. Or maybe we could see if they'd like to do a tie-in thing together? I have a friend that I met at Alisa's, and she works at the new Disney Store in the Glendale Galleria. She's actually good friends with a manager of the Toys 'R' Us over in Puente Hills, so maybe that could help us?

But okay, so, maybe it's like a game show mixed with a kid's show? Do they have those? Okay, so my giraffe. I'm calling her "Geena" for now. I was thinking of just going with "Cindy the

Giraffe," but I know a lot of companies like the alliteration thing for like, marketing and stuff, so I think Geena works. Plus, if I get Family Ties, maybe she, well, I, could end up becoming a recurring character if it goes, like, really well. So in that case, maybe we go through with the name change? I'd be a bigger name, then, so "Geena Giraffe" would be an easier sell. Not that I'd want to do this forever, obviously. Family Ties would be huge, and I know all about spin-off potential, so I don't want to pigeonhole myself into this kid's show thing, just—just in case, you know? So I'm thinking we go into Family Ties with Geena Dylan.

[SIPPING DRINK]

CINDY: For the name change, I mean. I think that has a good ring to it. Better than Cindy Dwyer, anyway. So, when you call me back, tell me your thoughts. Anyway, I'm thinking "Geena Giraffe" as, like, this game show host, and the kids are doing trivia in the first part, so I ask, like, um, "Which of these animals is a mammal?" And then we show a few different animals in the studio and then do a lesson on whichever one is the right answer, and the kids get points. Then there's a big challenge at the end between the two kids with the most points! It could take place in, like, wherever giraffes live? In a cave or something? Well, the showdown could be in the giraffe cave, or whatever. Now if we can get that Toys 'R' Us sponsorship, this would be a great place for them to give out some gift packages or something. So that's just the rough pitch. But we can talk about the details when I see you next. I'd love to set up a meeting again. Been a while since the last one, and I just want to make sure everything's all right on my end, just because there's a bit of paperwork I still haven't got and I want to make sure I gave you the right address. I'd be mortified if I got anything wrong here. One of my coworkers who's also out here to try and do some acting, he's from—

[PHONE PULLS AWAY. CINDY SNEEZES.]

CINDY: Excuse me. He's from Omaha, not too far from where my family is actually. But he said he thought it was a little weird that your process involves payment before contracts are finalized? I guess his agent does things a bit different, but I told him about how the money covers some processing fees and that you said it was pretty standard. I think he just felt like I should follow up with you, just in case. You hear these, like, horror stories of actors being taken advantage of, but I told him how you said you could set up the Family Ties audition so he would know you're the real deal. Oh! I also think I have the perfect song for the introduction to Geena Giraffe! It goes like this, and I'll just go ahead and do the voice I've been practicing for this character. Actually, though, I haven't practiced singing in the voice, so I'll just do the voice.

[THROAT CLEARING]

CINDY [IN VOICE OF GEENA GIRAFFE]: Come on kids, come on folks! Time for some trivia and some jokes! Questions come in all shapes and sizes, try and win some Toys 'R' Us prizes!
CINDY: Now, of course, we might have to change that line if we aren't able to get the Toys 'R' Us sponsorship right away...

CINDY [IN VOICE OF GEENA GIRAFFE]: Come play with me, Geena Giraffe! Play a fun game and have a little laugh!

CINDY: So, I don't know, that's... that's just a rough go at it. I think having the music will help. I know you'd mentioned working with a cousin of Billy Joel? So maybe, I don't know, I don't want to, like, rule him out as a potential. Well, that's all I've got for this call, Linda. Like I said earlier, I do think they're going to shut off my line this week, so if you get this call, or any of the other calls, just go ahead and call me at work. I'm at Alisa Thai Deli, that's 2810 West 9th Street, Los Angeles, California, and that phone number is 213-384-7049. So… yeah! Just call there and ask to speak to Cindy. Hope to hear from you soon about Family Ties, or the contracts, or just… anything! Thanks, Linda! Have a great weekend. If I don't hear from you, I'll call back Monday. Thanks, Linda!

[PHONE CLICKS. TAPE CLICKS.]

14.
12:47 A.M., SUNDAY, JULY 10, 2011

MACHINE: One new message from Sunday, July 10, 12:47 A.M.

[BEEP]

JASON: Joey! JOOOOEEEYYYYY! Dude, it's Jason. I'm—

[MUFFLED NOISES]

JASON: Hold on! I'm on the phone!

[MUFFLED NOISES]

JASON: I'm out at Billy Joe's with with Ben and Chris—

[MUFFLED NOISES]

JASON: No, I'm—no, I'll be over in a sec.

[MUFFLED NOISES]

JASON: Joey! Just wanted to say, what's uuuup, what's good? We all wish you came through tonight, bro! Fourth of July got mad crazy last weekend! I was fuckin' trashed. Can't even remember most of what happened after, like... I don't know if that's why you didn't come out tonight. Like, I know we were all pretty drunk, so you must have been, too, don't know if you weren't trying to be, like, hungover like that again or if something, like, happened. If something like, fuckin', went down between us that I don't remember. Not like—

[MUFFLED NOISES]

JASON: Hold on! Fuck.

[MUFFLED NOISES]

JASON: Not like I'm saying anything even did go down. Remember when Ben, fuckin', knocked the fuck out of Ace at the Myrtle house last summer? That shit was wild. I mean, Ace had a black eye and wasn't even pissed. That shit was mad funny. So yeah, I was just so blacked out that I barely even remember going to the car with you. That shit is just, like, barely in my mind.

Honestly, I was just calling to see if you even remember what we were talking about? Probably just some dumb shit. Me and Chris were all like, quoting The Hangover 2 to Jessie and Sam and they were like, "shut up, you are so dumb," and we were like, dying. Just dumb shit. So yeah, if you remember anything dumb, I was probably just being funny. Like, I don't know, I kinda remember being in your car? Just like, sitting there, like being awkward. We were probably just there to smoke, I mean, I know you said there wasn't any weed. All I'm sayin' is—

[MUFFLED NOISES]

JASON: We were on the swim team for four years. I think if one of us, fuckin', as a joke… like, how is that different than any of the times we were in the showers? Fuck, I'm—I don't know dude, I'm pretty drunk now, too. All I remember is we were in the car joking around for a little bit, so if that's why you're not here, I just want to say, like, I don't even remember anything, and I'm sure you don't remember anything, and no one even noticed we were gone for… Fuck, I don't even know how long we were gone. So yeah, neither remember anything, so if you get this and you're still out or up or whatever, there's a dope DJ here tonight and Jessie brought Tasha and she looks so fuckin' hot dude, I'm definitely trying to hook up. With her. So I'll def be here for a while if you want to come through and have a wingman. Could be cool to hang or whatever.

[PHONE CLICKS]

15.
10:54 P.M., SATURDAY, SEPTEMBER 13, 2008

MACHINE: One new message from Saturday, September 13, 10:54 P.M.

[BEEP]

DENNIS: Um, yeah, hi there. I believe I've reached the executive manager's line, here—to be frank, there were a few too many options the phone-robot menu gave me, so I'm not positive I picked the right one. Anyway, Dennis Travioli. I'm calling with H&B Elevators here in Minneapolis. I was at the show tonight here at the Guthrie Theater. First time in the new space, and it looks wonderful, I must say. And for my maiden voyage to be an Arthur Miller show, well that's just too sweet. I myself love Arthur Miller. I actually have a, well, a pretty funny Arthur Miller story for ya. In 1992, I—oh, well, ya know I should probably get to business first.

Like I said, my name is Dennis Travioli, I'm with H&B Elevators and wanted to talk to you about the elevators you got here in the theater. You went with the Kone Ecodiscs, which is a great choice, you're seeing that all up and down town nowadays. So I took myself on a little tour to check out these two sets of elevators you have during intermission. I figured I might as well, since with those bathroom lines and all, there's no way I'm making it back to my seat in time if I had tried to use the men's room. What can you do to fix that? I'm sure you don't want to put another bathroom in since you just finished construction on the new place, but, I don't know. Could be an idea. If you weren't satisfied with the bathroom job the first time around, I have a connection over at Saint Paul Plumbing, Heating & Air. I did make my way to the latrine before the show and I noticed a few of the toilets in the men's room had slow flush cycles. Suzanne told me the women's room toilets seemed good, but I can't always trust her to do a proper inspection, and, you know, couldn't go in there myself.

Anyway, the elevators: the first one, southeast wall, the one that goes from floors one to five, really flies. I mean that baby is smooth. No notes. But the second one, going from, uh, sorry, let me check—

[SHUFFLING PAPERS]

—okay, yeah, goes from floors five to nine, that one has a lag. It should not be that much slower than the first one. Extremely disorienting. You get yourself an elderly old lady in there, she could get knocked clear out. You must get that fixed as soon as possible. A-S-A-P. I can get my team in there to look at that, or you can call me directly at 612-873-9212.

[PAUSE. EXHALE.]

Anyways, I'd love to talk some Arthur Miller now that I got the ol' ups and downs out of the way! Just about always been a fan of the man. I read Death of a Salesman in high school. Actually played Biff in a performance when I was in college!

In 2002, I don't know if you were working here at the time, but Arthur Miller himself was in town here because he'd picked the Guthrie Theater to premiere his play, Resurrection Blues. I was so excited, even took off work to go to his conference. I have to be honest, don't remember too much about the play itself, because meeting him was so much more exciting! Whoops, spoiled my own damn story.

So I went to the conference, actually left my copy of Salesman on my table at home. But I did have my copy of A View From the Bridge, must have left it in my bag. Wasn't anything special, the Penguin Plays print from, uh, let me see here, 1983 or thereabouts. After the conference, I got to meet Mr. Miller—got him to sign my book! Very nice man. A bit distracted, but I understood, of course. I told him how honored I was to play Biff back in college and how I'd love to be in the play again one day, maybe even in this here theater. He nodded and said, "Best of luck!" Best of luck, from Arthur Miller to ol' Dennis.

I don't know if you know this or not, but the Guthrie Theater did a production of Salesman in 2004. Two years later and I was still riding high off of Mr. Miller's kind words, just had to audition. I was, well, I was a little bit too old, 'round 40 years old at that point, but I really gave it my all. My wife, Suzanne, always tells me I have a little baby face—and that's now, so a few years ago I bet I looked even younger. But I didn't get the part, as the tragedy goes.

You can see why it was a laugh for me, that View From the Bridge was being performed here now. The very play I had signed by Arthur Miller himself in this—well the former version of—this very theater. After I got done with the elevators, I tried to find the director to show him my signed play. Thought that'd be exciting, maybe inspirational. I must say, if I'm being completely honest, that this play was the worst Arthur Miller adaptation I've ever seen here at the Guthrie Theater. It was just horrible. I'm sorry if you specifically had anything to do with that. I actually didn't try out for this one, and I have to say that I believe I made the right decision. I wish you best of luck with the rest of this play's run, but...

Anyway, please contact me about the elevator speed discrepancies. I want the best for the stage, of course, but I'm even more concerned with safety. Again, my number is 612-873-9212. Just say you're calling about the Kone Ecodiscs at the Guthrie Theater, I'll know exactly what you mean. Alrighty there, have a good night, or whenever you get this message. And if this message is being left on the wrong machine, please direct this information to the proper person. My name is Dennis Travioli.

Thanks.

[PHONE CLICKS]

16.
6:18 A.M., WEDNESDAY, MAY 20, 2009

MACHINE: One new message from Wednesday, May 20, 6:18 A.M.

[BEEP]

HECTOR: Hey, is this Jeffrey? This is Hector, I was at your crib a few days ago to pick up that DVD player. Well I, um… bro, you left a movie in there. I didn't notice at first 'cause I didn't turn it on for a couple days after I bought it from you, but then I plugged it in and saw what you left in there…

[PAUSE]

HECTOR: I mean, you can do whatever, bro, but maybe be more careful about where you leave your shit, you know? I just wanted a cheap DVD player, I didn't want to see that shit. I don't know, like, what to do now. I'm not showing anybody or anything, I'm not like that, I just feel weird having seen it. I feel, like, dirty. I mean, you do you, but…

[PAUSE]

HECTOR: Do you want it back or something? I don't know. I think it should just be thrown away. I don't mean to judge, bro, I've seen some shit, so I'm not stupid or anything. But that seemed, like, dangerous. I guess I just wanted to call and say to be careful? I don't know you like that, I don't really know you at all except for when I seen you the other day, but I still think you should think about this a little bit, bro. I'm just going to throw it away. You don't need to call me back or anything, If you want to call back you can, I guess, I don't know. I feel weird, bro. It's okay, though. I think you're gonna be all right, Jeffrey. Maybe you just are lonely or some shit. I've been there. I haven't been where you been, but you know what I mean.

I'm gonna go now. You don't need to, like, be embarrassed or anything, like I said, I'm not going to say anything or show anyone, I'm just gonna throw this shit away. That's for the best. Okay. You don't need to call me back. Hope everything's okay, Jeffrey.

[PHONE CLICKS]

17.
11:03 P.M., THURSDAY, OCTOBER 18, 1990

MACHINE: One new message from Thursday, October 18, 11:03 P.M.

[BEEP]

HARRISON: Patrick, this is Harrison Corts. I'm going to make this very quick. I'm calling on behalf of a client whom I will not be naming here on this call, but on whom you are claiming to have some salacious...

Patrick, we're going to go ahead and nip this right in the bud. You don't have shit. OK? Nothing. What you have does not even warrant this call, which is in fact not happening. OK? What. You saw what, exactly? What are you claiming that you saw? You saw two people having a cordial lunch together. Can you, in the court of law, say that these people were even at lunch together? LA is a small town, my friend. You run into people. So let's start there, you... Patrick, I'm trying to hold it together, but frankly—you want to run a story that a person had lunch and saw someone out and about? Great. So, let me get this straight, when you're out having a salad on a Tuesday afternoon and you see—

[PAGES FLIPPING]

HARRISON: Eric and Molly's babysitter at the same restaurant, you don't say hello? It's a crime to say hello to your child's former babysitter now? Is that what you're pushin'? Basic cordiality is now a crime? Interesting! Interesting.

You stupid fuck.

[SIGH]

HARRISON: You seem to think it's a story that the man who was this close to being People Magazine's Sexiest Man Alive two months ago said hello to a former babysitter. A former employee? It was an alleged affair. AL-LEG-ED! Alleged by who? Oh that's right, your absolute shit tabloid rag. Never confirmed. And you can't expect me to believe that the bitter ex-wife of a notable actor and humanitarian who is making a very public display of dissatisfaction with the considerable amount of money she got in a divorce that she pushed is a credible source for this. Are you kidding me? Let me ask your ex-wife who she decided you were fucking after seeing you photographed with some ditz from halfway across the fucking Dodger Stad—

[LOUD KNOCK. MUFFLED NOISES.]

HARRISON [MUFFLED]: Yeah. Is there a 7-Up in here? Goddamnit. No. Keep the change.

[SHUFFLING SOUNDS]

HARRISON: Listen. I know you don't have shit, but people are gonna believe what they want. I need those pictures to go away. And let's be clear, here: she didn't start babysitting full-time for the family until she was 19, so these heinous and libelous accusations are absolutely false and unfounded and if you print anything with the implication, and I'm not even going to name it, but if you print any of those innuendos again you will be hearing again from the legal team. You don't want that heat right now, Patrick. Got it? Legal bullshit aside, how about you consider being a decent fucking person here. What's your angle? What's your endgame? A few copies sold and a family ruined over a story no one ever confirmed? You know there's kids caught up in all this, right? Kids, Patrick. How would you like it if I went up to, uh, Molly and Derek with a picture that looked like you were kissing their babysitter? I don't think you'd like that. So just drop it. I'm ending this message... actually, I can't end a message that doesn't exist. So listen, you vulturous fuck, call me back, call the payphone number I gave you at—

[SHUFFLING]

HARRISON: 11:50 tonight. OK? I may have a gift for you depending on how deeply fucking apologetic you are for making me make this call that I'm not making right now. Think clearly before you call, OK? I don't want to go outside just to hear something ridiculous.

[PHONE CLICKS. TAPE CLICKS.]

18.
7:52 P.M., THURSDAY, FEBRUARY 11, 1988

MACHINE: One new message from Thursday, February 11, 7:52 P.M.

[BEEP]

BARBARA: Hello? Is this—am I recording now? Okay, I think I'm recording now. So I'll, like, start talking.

[THROAT CLEARING]

BARBARA: Hiiii. My name is Barbara Jensen, pleasure to be talking to you, Mr. Warneke. Or, like, to your machine. A little background on me, for you: I've been in Bellevue for, well, about 10 years, so I've been reading the Bellevue Reporter for like, some time now. When I saw you became the, uh, manager? Manager-editor? last year, I started thinking of some ideas to maybe give you to add some new, like, flash to the paper. I'm not a professional writer, by any means, but I definitely have some, well I've been told I have some really cool ideas. I don't have a, like, super-extensive resume, but I have worked on some Hollywood movies, so I think people in Bellevue have definitely gravitated towards my energy and my, like, mind. You may have heard me do a reading of some of my poems at the library? The crowds are small, but like, really respond to my work.

So yeah, I was thinking of some fun ideas for the paper. I guess I should mention I'm originally from California. I know what you're thinking, Mr. Warneke, but I am spoken for and am no longer the little babe on the beach. Do you know my husband, Rodney? I know smart people run together, he's a professor at U of N. That's actually why we moved here. Our son Dean was only eight when we left Santa Monica, he never got to have the teen beach years like I did. Rodney wasn't a beach boy himself, he was more of a holed-up-in-the-lab type of guy. That's sort of why I liked him to begin with. I guess I thought I could get him to climb out and see the sun at some point.

Anyway, my ideas: my son, Dean, he's in his second year at Iowa State now, and he called me today and you wouldn't believe it! Kent—can I call you Kent? Well, Kent, I don't know if you follow the weather, but today in Ames it was negative 15 degrees Fahrenheit! That is cold! When Dean told me that, it really hit me. People need to feel warm, these winters are just too much. So, Kent, what if I wrote some stories about the California beaches for the Reporter? I already have a name for it! We can call it "Shories, by Barbara." Do you get it? Shore-stories! Shories! I think people here in the, like, middle of winter would love to feel like they're on a beach. I have the experience, I can do this, I know this. When I tell stories at the library readings, there are attendees who are, like, really pulled in! Ok, so like, here's the first story, or "shorie," that I thought of:

There's this guy named Buddy. He's a surfer, and the girl he's going with, Linda, is just a regular beach babe who like, loves California. Then one day she meets this guy named Daniel, and he's not a surfer but he loves the skyline and that's why he was at the beach. So then Linda falls in love with Daniel and leaves Buddy and then moves far away so Buddy stops surfing because he only did it to impress Linda but now she's not on the beach so the world without her, like, falls apart.

[PAUSE. SIPPING WATER.]

BARBARA: Or another idea is this girl named Mary is a lifeguard on the beach, and one day, she swims out very far to save this guy who is, like, flailing all around, but then it turns out when she gets to him that he actually can swim and he was just trying to get her attention. I have a million others, Kent. I spend these horrible winter days in Nebraska dreaming up these shories, and I think the people here would really appreciate them. I don't expect an answer right away, but I do think that winter is really the best time to print these. I mean, I've met some people here, a lot of people actually, who have never been to California at all. Let alone the beaches in Santa Monica.

I'll just share one last idea. It's about a little kid who's on the street, he's walking around and he's lost and he just listens to the waves. He walks toward the water and finds his family and they're like, it's okay, kid, you're home now.

I'm going to go ahead and get out of your hair now, I'm sure you've got a million calls like this to go through. I'm here at the house most days, so if you'd like to discuss this idea further, please call! Rodney wasn't completely sold on the idea. But like I said, he never cared about the beach like I do. Okay Kent, hopefully talk to you soon. Stay warm!

[PHONE CLICKS. TAPE CLICKS.]

19.
2:11 P.M., WEDNESDAY, JANUARY 11, 2018

VOICEMAIL: One new message from Wednesday, January 11, 2:11 P.M.

[BEEP]

ALEXANDER: Hello Alice, it is Alexander, from the Regal Customer Service. We were speaking like it's, uh, maybe one hour before about your gift card. Okay, we just checked that. That gift card, uh, blocked from the, uh, the company. We are not able to unblock that. You, basically, you need to go to the door theater, ask them for empty gift card. If they will not give you empty gift card, just purchase gift card card for like, let's say fifteen dollars, something like that, and call us back and... unfortunately, I am done in my shift right now, you can call us back...

[PAPERS SHUFFLING]

ALEXANDER: ...in two days. I will be on my shift in two days, or, each representative knows about it, no worries. Yes. Ask that person please to take your new card number and we will add twenty five dollars to that card. Okay? Sorry for that inconvenience, you have a great day and enjoy the movies. Okay. Thank you, bye-bye.

[PHONE CLICKS]

20.
11:07 P.M., MONDAY, MARCH 4, 2013

MACHINE: One new message from Monday, March 4, 11:07 P.M.

[BEEP]

VINNY: Listen, I know you're probably freaking the fuck out right now, but listen: It's fine, it's gonna be fine. I fucked everything up, yeah, but look—this shit wasn't my fault.

[MUFFLED NOISES]

VINNY: TAXI! TA—fuck.

[MUFFLED NOISES]

VINNY: Listen, you Russian fuck. I know you were at my house tonight, which is why I WASN'T THERE! I can explain everything. Don't... I wouldn't, just don't come looking for me right now. I'll be around. What day is it?

[PAUSE]

VINNY: It's Monday. Okay, it's Monday? I'm two days late, that's not the end of the fuckin' world, now, is it?

[MUFFLED NOISES]

VINNY: Taxi! What the—

[MUFFLED NOISES]

VINNY: Vlad. Big bad Vlad. When I saw your ASSHOLE friend Ivan, or whatever the fuck, I told him I would have the money by Saturday UNLESS I could get you everything, interest included, by Sunday. Yesterday, right? So listen. I had it. I had the money. I had the 5k from that fuckin' dentist's game two weekends ago, which you and I both know was absolute bullshit anyways. And I had the 12k I owed you for the shit with Rosenthal and his butt-buddy. That put me 7k under where I needed to be. So I figure, what the fuck, I'll wait and see if I can come up with the rest by tonight. That's why I wasn't around Saturday, but thanks to my fuckin' doorbell camera I saw you got my note about Sunday, right? SO, here I am, havin' a few vodka sodas or whatever the fuck and remember that your beloved New York Knickerbockers are playing my humble Miami Heat. In the spirit of friendly competition, my dear Vlad, in honor of me gettin you your, and I'm using your very generously here, but in honor of me gettin' you your money, I go ahead and make a little wager on this game—

[COUGHING]

VINNY: So I bet on the Heat. I bet the over on my sweet King James getting 25 and I bet a little somethin' for you here, the over on Melo getting 30. MEELLOOOOOOO!!!

So I'm at a hotel, sippin' away and watching YOUR money pile up. I'm doing you a huge favor. Heat win. Fourteen in a row baby, LeBron gets 29, Melo gets 32. Boom. I'm out, you're up, we kiss and make up.

[PAUSE]

VINNY: This is where things got fucked up. This is where I SHOULD HAVE CALLED and told you to pick up your fuckin' money.

So, right before, at this little hotel bar, there's one other guy there. This black guy, Alonzo. We're watching the game together, having a good time, you know? I don't tell him how much I put down, but he picks up that I have some skin on it, so he's bustin' my balls. All in good fun. So I win, WE win, and I buy him a drink and we get talkin'. Where else am I going to go? Find out this guy's here cause his kid has a movie at the Miami International Film Festival, or works at it, I don't fuckin' know.

Turns out he's from Minnesota, the black guy. So we get back to talkin' hoops. Heat are playing the Wolves the next night, tonight. So I say, fuck it, let's meet up and watch this game, too! Vlad, this is where it gets interesting. He tells me there's this skinny Russian prick on the Wolves. I say no way. Now I'm thinking about this game. So we're sittin' around, and I'm thinking about this Russian, like this shit's an omen. I gotta bet on this game, beyond the friendly wager between me and black Alonzo.

[SIPPING DRINK]

VINNY: So I call up Richie, you know Richie, and I ask about this game. I ask what he thinks about this Russian, Alexey Shved. He doesn't know much, but I'm thinkin', who's ever heard of a Russian in the NBA? I do a parlay right there. I take the under on LeBron getting 30. I take the Heat winning and I take the over on this Russian getting 15. That's nothin'. Love's out, Pek is out, that big fuck. So I think he's got this, points gotta come from somewhere. I bet it all—minus 2k, you told me to always clean 2k off the top of any winnings, and I listen to you Vlad, but I bet the rest. Then I pass the fuck out, sleep for like 15 hours, wake up, do whatever all day, check my security cam to see your creepy Russian ass hanging outside my door, then I go meet up with Alonzo to watch this game that's gonna make you and me both a hefty fuckin' coin.

Right away, and I'm gonna be honest with you Vlad, I didn't feel right. I didn't like it. This guy Alonzo says he's gotta make a call right at the beginning of the game and then he leaves. Doesn't come back. Feel like I'm some dumb broad bein' stood up. So listen, you can guess the rest. Heat win. Good to go, 15 straight muthafucka. LeBron goes under 30. Boom. But this Russian fuck, Shved, fucks me. Takes a 3, makes it and gets fouled, goes for the 4-point play. Makes this free throw that would put him at 16 points. We're fuckin' golden. I'm elated. I'm suckin' your dick after a night at the theater. Then what? Then the refs wave this shit off, so it's a foul ON Shved. Take away the 3, no chance for the free point. Your Russian boy let us down, Vlad! I put everything on this. It was spiritual! I don't think any Russian had ever been in the NBA, so when I heard Russian player, I had to do it. Vlad, I had to. TAXI!

[MUFFLED NOISES]

VINNY: You still on duty? Just drive for a minute…

[MUFFLED NOISES]

VINNY: Then I remember, and this killed me, but I remember fuckin' Mozgov! Your own Knicks had a Russian, and I forgot and I fucked up because of it. I'm gonna need more time. I need a few days. I still got that 2k. I can turn this into what you need. I'm going to have it all, plus interest, plus a little cherry on top for your Russian ass. Trust me, Vlad. It's coming back the fuck around.

[PHONE CLICKS]

21.
4:46 P.M., WEDNESDAY, AUGUST 15, 2012

VOICEMAIL: One new message from Wednesday, August 15, 4:46 P.M.

[BEEP]

ISAIAH: Ay, sis. I'm just callin' to let you know I probably won't make dinner tonight. I'm at the storage unit, and it's gonna take longer than we thought. Weird as hell bein' here, goin' through Pops's old shit. Mostly junk, lot of computers that are probably too old to turn on. A few photo albums I'll bring by when I come over. Him and Mom look mad young, it's crazy. There's also a bunch of tapes. A VCR and a TV, too. You know Pops. So I watched this one from some party. I think it might have been, like, my fourth birthday, before you and Susie were born. Every time I fast forwarded and stopped I saw Aunt Dinah asking Uncle Bill, "How much you gonna drink?" And each time he just was shakin' his head, looking drunk as hell. By the end, he was just dead asleep on the couch. I was crackin' up.

[LAUGHTER]

ISAIAH: Billy was there, too, with his jheri-curl and his Raiders hat, like he was Eazy-E. My little ass was cryin' every time the camera turned to me. Grandma Clara would try and get me to stop crying by sittin' me on her lap. That just made me cry even more.

[LAUGHTER]

ISAIAH: It's nice, being around all this stuff. Been a minute since we saw Mom's side of the family. I'm still mad Billy didn't come to Pops's funeral. We were all at Uncle Bill's, even after all that mess.

I saw these boots down here that Pops brought back from

Desert Storm. I don't know if he ever told you about them. They're black on the bottom, jet black. I used to think that was just part of the boot, but he told me that in Saudi, there were mad bombs that blew up oil wells and shit. He said it was so bad it would look like it was raining oil. Spilled oil was all you could see for miles in some places. That's where the black on his boots came from.

I was picturing young Pops, lookin' like he did in these pics, out there in the desert. Walking around with these boots and those big ass glasses and seeing bombs and camels and shit. Then I realized he wasn't on that tape I was watchin'. I checked the date on the bottom of the screen and realized he must have been deployed. Weird to think about. I was crying on Grandma Clara's lap while he was shoveling shit and walking around fiery ass oil fields with these boots on. Probably only, like, 25. My age now.

[PAUSE. SIGH.]

ISAIAH: I'ma keep these if that's cool with you. There's not too much else over here, buncha junk. Found his old Bible in the same box as some dusty ass Playboys. You know Pops. I still haven't seen that box of toys you were talkin' about. I'ma keep lookin, though. Sorry I couldn't come through tonight. I'll see y'all this weekend.

[PHONE CLICKS]

22.
2:11 P.M., THURSDAY, APRIL 30, 2020

MACHINE: One new message from Thursday, April 30, 2:11 P.M.

[BEEP]

GLADYS: —ello? Hello? Richard? Hello? Richard? SIRI, CALL RICHARD!

[MUFFLED NOISES]

GLADYS: It looks like—

[MUFFLED NOISES]

GLADYS: Richard, it says I am calling you now. Can you hear me? It's Mom. Richard? If you can hear me, please say something.

[MUFFLED NOISES]

GLADYS: It still says you're here, speaker?

[MUFFLED NOISES. PHONE SWITCHES TO SPEAKER.]

GLADYS: Richard, can you hear me now? I pushed on the speaker. Can you hear me? I want to do the video, how do I do the video call? I am going to hang up and call you again. If you can hear me, I wanted to tell you that the virus has now killed both Nellie and Irene. No visitors are allowed to come to the home, so do not try to come to the home. Do you remember Irene? She was in the room a few doors away. She—Richard? Is that you? I thought I heard you. Irene was in the room a few doors away. Her son was the one who was on the television program. Such a nice man! Pray for Irene's family. Nellie never had her family here, she was a very mean woman. She never wanted to play gin rummy. I told her happy birthday and she never said thank you. Well, it's still sad. I hope she had the Lord in her heart, though it did not seem like she did. I'm going to hang up now Richard. Please do not come here this week. Tell Rebecca do not come here either. Call me back so I—

[PHONE CLICKS]

23.
3:47 P.M., TUESDAY, AUGUST 28, 2007

MACHINE: One new message from Tuesday, August 28, 3:47 P.M.

[BEEP]

CHRIS: Hey, Sarah! It's your Uncle Chris. It's, uhhh, somewhere around... 3:40 on Tuesday. I don't know the date. It's today, I don't know. Anyway, wanted to call and see how you're doin', check in on how the trip back to school went. Not just a freshman anymore! That's great. Now you can beat the kids up, light their hair on fire, whatever you girls in college do nowadays— What? Okay, yeah. Aunt Talia says hello.

Wanted to call and say hi, and miss you, and I had two things I wanted to mention. Number one: I saw the new Rush Hour this weekend. Didn't think it was very good. You can skip it, I know you like the artsy-fartsy stuff now anyway. Even I have a limit to the bad movies I can handle. Maybe your fancy taste is rubbing off on me.

Okay, number two, and this is a big one: I've been doing lots of thinking, and I'm sure your mom has told you, but I still haven't got a job. That interview I had in the city a few weeks ago didn't pan out. Went with someone with a better degree, probably. But, so that got me thinkin', what am I going to do next? Been out of work for a few months, as you know, so somethin's gotta happen. But this weekend I had a huge idea, and I want you to get in on it if you're up to it. I was watching some TV, and have you seen this show called Cash Cab? It's just great. This driver picks people up and then does trivia with them, and they win money. Nice and simple and fun.

Now here's what I'm thinking: What if we do this in Albany? It was a party town back when I was in school. It's still a party town now! People are taking cabs to get to the bars and party houses and stuff, and my friend Jake, you remember him, he owns a used car lot and he said he could get me a van for pretty cheap. If we get a place in Albany to sponsor us, like, we paint their name on the van, whatever they want, maybe they'd pay for the van and could put up some prize money?

So we'd pick kids up, and I would have trivia questions for them, and if they get them right, they get a cheaper toll, and the longer the go they could end up with a free ride, maybe even win cash on top of that and——What? No, it's——no. By the fridge. Yeah.

Sorry about that. So, I do the driving and trivia and you can do the filming? I don't know where it would play just yet. I have a friend who said he could help me with some website stuff if we wanted to go that route. Remember those cool little movies BMW had on their website? Maybe you don't. You liked them, at the time. I think it'll be fun to work together! It'll be like when I used to watch you at the shop, except this time you'll actually be useful. Kidding, of course.

Let me know, Sar. I think I have to get a different license before I do this, technically, so we've got some time to work out the details. Don't tell your mom. I don't want her yelling at me, acting like I'm going to mess up your school stuff. I take that very seriously. I mean, of course I need a job. This would be a job. I'm not embarrassed to admit that my idea that I came up with would be a good thing for me! BUT——let's not forget that it'd be helping you, too! You get professional TV show experience and have a degree? Are you kidding? You'll be head of ABC, or CBS, or whatever. Okay. Take some time to think on it in between your French black and white movies and call me back. Love you, kiddo.

[PHONE CLICKS]

24.
11:19 P.M., THURSDAY, FEBRUARY 15, 1996

MACHINE: One new message from Thursday, February 15, 7:15 P.M.

[BEEP]

TRAVIS: Yo, Nathaniel. It's Travis. Just got confirmation—oh, if this is someone other than Nathaniel listening, please stop now. This is private information. Thanks.

[SHORT PAUSE]

TRAVIS: Anyway, my guy confirmed that The Manzini family is having a huge engagement celebration for Nicole at Lombardo's tomorrow night. It was already gonna be packed 'cause it was Valentine's Day yesterday, so people will go there for, like, their dates and shit tomorrow. You know, since it was on a weekday. I worked it last year, it was the same deal and it was fuckin' packed. Back to the Manzini's. You know them, mad rich, but two years ago, Francesca got married. She was, like, the middle child, and Donny went crazy, pulled out all the stops, spent like fuckin' crazy at the dinner and even bought everyone in the restaurant a drink at one point.

So I'm thinking, Nicole is his oldest, he's gotta throw a way crazier party for her, right? If you got the private room at Lombardo's filled up, and everyone else there is for Valentine's dates and everything gets more expensive, like, for specials and shit, and everyone is buyin', like, a bottle of wine or something, they're gonna be swimming in it. 'Cause I told you, Lombardo's is cash only. You hardly ever see that shit at a place that nice these days. Everyone in this restaurant's buying overpriced meals, drinking, weekend shit, plus an engagement party? Probably, like, 50 people working, all paid in cash. So late at night, when they're closed up, they got one person who goes into the back room to lock up the cash—actually, since it's Friday, it'll probably be most of the cash from the week. Fuck! I didn't even think of that. Damn.

Okay, here's what I'm thinking. Write this down, I don't wanna have to call you back. I live at 416 Traverse Boulevard, pick me up there at exactly 10:45. Then we're gonna drive to 45 Virgil Ave—that's my boy's house—we're gonna park in his driveway because his family is out of town and it's right near Lombardo's. Bring a blanket, 'cause it's fuckin' freezing and you can't sit there with the car running the whole time. When we park, I'll leave and go behind some of the houses toward the back of the restaurant. No one will be outside, so I don't have to worry about anybody seeing me. I'll go through the back when it's just the last person closing up. Actually, that'll probably be later. I don't want to stand outside for too long, it's gonna be like five degrees out. Fuck, actually, pick me up at 11. Once I go in, I'll get whoever's there to keep the safe open, get the cash, run the fuck back to the driveway, and then we'll fuckin' book it. I'm not gonna, like, kill anyone, I got this police baton that I'll just, like, swing at someone's head mad hard. No gunshots or anything, but we still gotta get out fast. So when I get back to the car we'll—hold on, lemme look at this map...

[PAPER SHUFFLING]

TRAVIS: So we'll take a right off Virgil on to Tacoma and then turn left down, uh, Colvin... and then my Mom's is right off of Traverse where we started. My guess is that if they get the cops to start looking that night, they'll come straight to my house 'cause the Lombardo's fuckin' hate me and will probably think it was me cause they've always fuckin' hated me. Whatever, fuck 'em. So I gotta get home quick, crawl back through my window and get in bed. Mom'll be in the living room, probably dead asleep with the TV on, so she won't even know I left. She can be my alibi, she won't even know I was gone. She'll vouch for me.

As for you, take the money and book a hotel or some shit. I don't know, you gotta start figuring shit out for yourself.

Like I said, don't call back or anything. Just write this all down and then erase this message. Don't pussy out. See you tomorrow at 10:45. I mean 11! Yeah, 11. Oh yeah, wear normal clothes, but like, dark. Okay.

[PHONE CLICKS. TAPE CLICKS.]

25.
3:33 P.M., WEDNESDAY, NOVEMBER 5, 1997

VOICEMAIL: One new message from Wednesday, November 5, 3:33 P.M.

[BEEP]

JAIME: Hi Philip, this is Jamie. I wanted to say hello since you weren't in school today and also let you know our printing box had eleven new pieces of paper in there. I wanted to read them to you so that you can print them tonight in case you are feeling better and come to school tomorrow. I'm going to get the box now.

[FOOTSTEPS, MUFFLED NOISES]

JAIME: Mom? Mom? Where's my backpack?

UNSPECIFIED: In the kitchen.

JAIME: I looked there already.

UNSPECIFIED: On the chair.

JAIME: Oh. Okay, found it.

[FOOTSTEPS, MUFFLED NOISES]

JAIME: Sit, Charlie. Sit. Good boy!

[MUFFLED NOISES]

JAIME: I found the box. The first thing is that Erin wants a picture of Tommy Pickles printed out. I told her if she wanted it in color it was ten cents instead of five cents, and she said okay, so can you print that one in color? Are you going to write this down? Because I can't call you back, and my Dad said he's not bringing home a printer from work, actually.

Shannon wants a picture of two horses. She didn't say if she wanted it in color or black and white, but since a lot of horses are black and white, I guess you can just print that one in black and white. That one is five cents.

Daniel asked for a picture of a truck. He just wrote down "truck," so I don't know what kind he wants. Just pick a red truck and print it in color. We can charge ten cents and he will have to pay. Eric K. wants a picture of Mark McGwire, but he said to make sure it's a Cardinals one. He said to print it in color, but my mom said Eric K. is poor so we can print it in black and white. Caitlyn R. also wants a picture of Tommy Pickles, so print two of those. Benjamin wants a picture of Goliath from Gargoyles. Hold on please, I have to go to the bathroom.

[MUFFLED NOISES. LONG PAUSE. TOILET FLUSHES.]

JAIME: Sorry, Philip. I have five more pictures to tell you about. Michael R. wants a picture of Lara Croft Tomb Raider. My Mom said I'm not allowed to play that, but when I went to Michael R.'s house I got to play it. Janet wants a picture of Ace Ventura in color. Oh yeah, and Michael R. wants it in black and white, even though my mom said he's rich. Are you writing all these down? Lana wants—

UNSPECIFIED: Jaime, it's time for homework.

[MUFFLED NOISES]

JAIME: Hold on, Mom. I have to tell Philip a few more things for our business.

[MUFFLED NOISES]

JAIME: Philip, I have to go in a second. Lana wants a picture of a golden retriever. Her dog died, that's probably why. Alex K. wants a picture of a hockey stick in black and white. Ashley wants a picture of her Grandma, but I don't think we can do that one. I don't know who her Grandma is, maybe you do. The last one is that Dan Lopez wants a picture of the Bible. I don't think they are very colorful, so I guess you can do black and white. Once you print all of them that will be—

[LONG PAUSE]

JAIME: Hold on please, Philip.

[LONG PAUSE]

JAIME: If you can find a picture of Ashley's grandma in color, we will make 95 cents. So for the whole week, we'll have—

[LONG PAUSE]

JAIME: two dollars and 15 cents. That is pretty good. Okay, Philip? Please remember to cut the website off of the bottom of the page and write the person on the back of the picture so that way we know what person gets the picture. If you can't do it tonight, please do it tomorrow because then the next day is Friday, and if we don't have it before the weekend everyone will be mad at you. I hope you aren't too sick. Goodbye, and don't call back 'cause I have to do homework now.

[PHONE CLICKS]

26.
10:36 A.M., THURSDAY, SEPTEMBER 20, 2001

MACHINE: One new message from Thursday, September 20, 10:36 A.M.

[BEEP]

DR. PETERS: Hello, Andrea, this is Dr. Peters at St. Vincent's Hospital. I'm calling at 10:36 on Thursday the 20th in regard to Anthony. Please come back to the hospital as soon as you get this. Thank you.

[PHONE CLICKS. TAPE CLICKS.]

27.
11:15 P.M., FRIDAY, JUNE 19, 2015

MACHINE: One new message from Friday, June 19, 2015, 11:15 P.M.

[BEEP]

MOM: Jeremy, this is your mother calling. It's now quarter-past 1:00, that's 1:15, and I'm just wondering where the HELL you are? Again and again with you, Jeremy. I don't know what I'm supposed to do at this point. What are you doing right now? Are you drinking? Even after...

[EXHALE]

MOM: ...even after your uncle was arrested? My own son, who I raised, who I fed from my breast, is out drunk driving. You won't remember this, but there was a time where we went to Richard Daniels's birthday party at Arnold's Fun Center. You took one look at the go-karts and immediately started grabbing my leg and saying you didn't want to drive, "Mommy, Mommy, I don't want to drive the car," that's what you were saying. And now look at you, drunk driving with God knows who! Not with Richard Daniels, I can tell you that! Janet tells me he's choosing between Harvard and Yale. Harvard! Yale! What a life!

Oh, Jeremy. Last weekend you almost missed curfew, too. I let it slide, and look what happened. Oh, I was planning a nice day for us tomorrow, too! I thought we'd go to Chadwick's for dinner, get the Asian chicken salad. I guess that's what I get for thinking things are on the up and up. It's been a good few weeks, but oh, I don't know.

[PAUSE. EXHALE.]

MOM: Is this because of your father?

[LAUGHING]

MOM: I'm just going to say it: I think you're smoking weed! Your friend "Stephanie" smelled like what I remember weed smelling like the other day, and I didn't say anything, but God curses me for holding my tongue, and I deserve it! I have a drunk-driving, pot-smoking, math-flunking son. What should I be doing differently, Jer? Are you unhappy in our home? I know it isn't perfect, but I do my best. I guess that's not enough.

I'll tell you something, and you're not going to like to hear it, but Renee from Bible study thinks I'm coddling you. Coddling. How do you like that? Everyone in the world thinks my son is a delicate little baby boy. Little do they know he's a drug-ridden alcoholic. I don't like having to do this Jeremy. I just th—

[PAUSE]

MOM [QUIETLY]: Wait, why does this clock say... Hold on...

[PAUSE]

MOM: Shit.

[MUFFLED NOISES]

MOM: Okay, you just walked in and you're not late. Just erase and ignore this, I love you sweetie!

[PHONE CLICKS]

28.
1:30 P.M., WEDNESDAY, MARCH 11, 1998

MACHINE: One new message from Wednesday, March 11, 1:30 P.M.

[TAPE CLICKS]

[LOUD ROCK MUSIC]

MARTY: Hey! This is Marty. I, uh, got your number from Jack.

[EXTENDED PAUSE]

MARTY: I just… this is kinda weird. I just wanted to call, well, because you were actually in my dream last night.

[NERVOUS LAUGH]

MARTY: Kind, of dumb, right? People hate hearing about someone else's "crazy little dream." But I felt like I should tell you, it's… We were together in kind of an "elephant graveyard" situation. Like, you know, from The Lion King? Like the place with the hyenas, where the light doesn't touch. Anyway, we were walking together, and it's all dusty and gray, and then, like, all of a sudden, I look over at you and you're wearing—and again, I know how dumb this sounds—but you're wearing this cream colored lace dress. It reminded me of this nightstand cloth my mom kept by her bed, actually.

So you're wearing this dress, and out of nowhere, you drop to the ground and start screaming. Like, really screaming. Like the kind of scream you hear from someone who just lost someone, the kind that sticks with you for a while afterward. You just start screaming, until you go, "I will… I WILL BE ALONE." And then… your eyes start bleeding. Like, really bleeding. Blood gushing from your eyes. Not in a cartoonish way, either, in a really violent and just, um, visceral way. It was so…

[EXTENDED PAUSE]

MARTY: ...horrifying. But not in the way you'd think it would be. Like, yeah, of course, the bleeding eyes and the desolate wastelands are scary. And there's some weird stuff that happens after with bones, but the thing that really got me, what I found really disturbing about the whole thing, was that it was like, completely erotic.

And don't get me wrong, I'm not some kind of creep who's into that sort of thing. I wouldn't even bring up the "E" word if I didn't feel it was completely necessary. And, I mean, it's not like I'm getting off on eye-gouging or whatever, I'm not into smut or anything like that. Can't stand that stuff, really. I've known people who are into that, so I've seen it, and it's absolutely not for me. But I can't get this dream out of my head, I really can't. It's just lingering there, I've been picturing you in that lace dress all day! It's having this profound physiological effect on me that I can't explain or understand. Even just talking about it now, I'm...

You ever have a dream, just a benign, regular dream, and you end up, like, subconsciously pinning an inappropriate emotional reaction to it? Like, I used to have this dream when I was a kid that I was going out for ice cream with my stepdad. I'd have it all the time, it was like one of those dreams where you're stuck in high school even though you know you're in your 30s.

But anyway, I would have this dream about getting ice cream with my stepdad. It would be at this spot, Mr. Ice's, a place a lot of us went to in the summer. We get up to the register, and he pays, and the second they hand me the cone, I'm hit with the deepest bolt of panic I've ever felt. Pure terror. I'd wake up screaming, sweating, there were times I even peed the bed—just a little bit—and whenever my mom would come to my room, I'd be so wound up and confused I could never tell her what was wrong. I really didn't know, I haven't suffered any ice cream-related trauma. So when she asked what was wrong, I just wouldn't say anything.

And then for weeks afterward, my mom gets on the phone with her friends, telling them Marty woke up screaming again and won't tell me why, and sometimes she'd blame my stepdad, and then they fight, and then everybody's as screwed up as I am just because I don't understand what's happening in my dreams, only they don't know that because I can't put it in words. So I think that's what's going with this dream and the elephant graveyard and the screaming and the bleeding eyes and me getting so hot about all of it. At least I hope so...

[SIGHS]

MARTY: Anyway, feels good to get this off my chest. Wish I'd been able to do that as a kid. Kind of a silly story. I can hear you just cracking up at this as I speak. Call me back if you get this, but if not, I'm super excited to start working together next week!

[PHONE CLICKS. TAPE CLICKS.]

29.
11:56 P.M., WEDNESDAY, DECEMBER 24, 1997

MACHINE: One new message from Wednesday, December 24, 11:56 P.M.

[TAPE CLICKS]

DAN: If anyone's listening, this is Dan, calling my own machine. It's Christmas Eve. If you're hearing this, it's because I'm dead. I'm in Milwaukee, at this fucking Hyatt downtown. My stay here got extended through the new year, and I just—I can't do this anymore. If you don't want to listen to this whole thing, I'll sum it up: I killed myself. Jumped off the roof of the Hyatt Regency in Milwaukee. It's not your fault or anything. Whoever's listening.

[SIPPING DRINK]

DAN: I read about this woman, Vesna, uh, Vulkovic? Or something. I think she was Russian. She was a flight attendant on this plane that had a terrorist on it, and a bomb exploded while the plane was in the air, and everyone died. Except for her! She fell, like, 30,000 fucking feet or whatever, and she was fine! I mean, not fine, but she didn't die—just broke a few bones. Got on TV, got a book deal. So I guess there's a chance I'll survive this, if she did. Wonder if she's still alive. I wonder if she thinks about it all the time. How could you not? But if you're listening to this, I'm definitely dead. So, good, I guess.

[SIPPING DRINK]

DAN: I've gained, like, thirty pounds since Grace broke things off. Which was, what, seven months ago? Probably why Margaret went home early. She said they gave her a break and sent her home for the holidays, but I think she just couldn't stand the sight of my fat fuckin'...

I try very hard to be nice and charming. In a platonic way, I'm not a creep or anything. But I think she thinks I want her, and so she's sizing me up, and she's just absolutely repulsed. Well she can go to hell. Bitch. Has arms that are too long for her body. She's not very confident, either. Very off-putting in general. And frankly, I think when you're working with managers like we do, you should have a good amount of confidence. The clients just don't respect her very much, even if they act like they do.

I don't know. I'm just miserable. Absolutely miserable. The clients don't respect me, either. Despite the fact that I've been working with them for over four years. Two years longer than Margaret, who they don't respect, but they do respect her more than me. I shouldn't have to be here for another two weeks. I hate this company. I hate this business. I need to be taken care of. I show up. I show up, and I need to be taken care of. How the fuck am I supposed to crawl out when I'm forty-grand in the—

[COUGHING]

DAN: —How the fuck did this happened? I really should just kill myself. Listen, I just, I'm drunk right now, too, so if I'm, I don't know, you know, that's why. Don't take me too seriously. Who am I talking to?

I spent a few hours at a bar called the Swingin' Door about a half mile from here. I had a few and shared some fries with a person who tried to kiss me outside the bar. I had to push them off and let them know I'm not gay, at all. Think I saw them follow me back to the hotel. I don't even want to leave in case they're waiting for me outside. Thank God I got booze yesterday. So I'll be stuck inside this fucking room on Christmas. I don't care, I'll leave. I have to. I'll ask the front desk for pepper spray.

Look, if you're listening, I'm not going to kill myself, okay? I'm just drunk and feel like shit and hate this job and this life and Margaret and I miss Grace, even though she was a liar and never believed in me or my potential, and I'm ready for something new, even though I know nothing new is coming, and I'm so far in the hole, and Mom and Dad won't speak to me, and I don't know how I'll make it through this year and I'm fat and ugly and haven't had sex in months and months and the only person who wants to fuck me is that old queen at the bar. Now that I'm thinking about it, I don't even know if I could get to the roof without some alarm going off. That'd be just perfect. The fire department would come and everybody'd get to see some fat, drunk loser waddling back down the stairs to his shit room on the fourth floor. Maybe I'll do it tomorrow. So if you get this message, and I am dead after all, I killed myself by jumping off the roof of the Hyatt Regency in downtown Milwaukee on Christmas Day. Not Christmas Eve.

[SIPPING DRINK. SIGHING.]

DAN: In second grade, before we went on winter break for the year, I sang the Heat Miser song from that fucking clay movie in front of the whole class. That's when I first started thinking about killing myself. I got halfway through the song and realized I didn't have a good voice. And not in, like, a funny or cute way. Nobody liked it. And I kept going. What a metaphor. Those kids had never looked shame in the eyes until then.

I bet Margaret wishes I was dead. She'd never say it, but she does. I see how she looks at me when I'm presenting. I bet the bartender at the Swingin' Door wishes I was dead, too. Just another traveling drunk who thinks he's Humphrey fuckin' Bogart because he's drinking with a tie on. You know, I don't even have a hobby. Who doesn't have a hobby? I don't like anything. I would try fishing. The last time I fished was with Uncle Tim when I was fifteen. I dropped his new pole off the side of the boat and he called me a prick. I didn't do it on purpose, I was a kid. He couldn't hide his complete and utter disdain for his own nephew. Why wouldn't they make fishing poles float? I'd try to drown myself but I bet I would just start floating. Plus I'm a great swimmer, so my powerful instincts would likely kick in.

Margaret goes rock climbing. That killed with the executives yesterday. They couldn't get enough. As if she's the first fucking woman to climb a rock. Dan, what do you do? Nothing, so I didn't know what to say. I pulled something out of my ass and said that I like trains, or some shit. Completely bombs, dead silence in the conference room. I wonder if Margaret made it home. I bet she'd survive a plane bombing.

[SIPPING DRINK]

DAN: She'd make it all about herself, I bet. She'd call that Russian woman and try and go on TV together, and they'd write a book, and everyone would love it. They'd love Margaret and Vesna and forget about the fat drunk who survived in the back of the plane. They'd probably wish I hadn't survived. I bet the kids from second grade would see me and remember when I sang that song and start laughing and tell their kids about what a loser I was. Fuck them. I'm just as good as Margaret and I'm not going to kill myself to just appease them. I've been working too hard for too long and not getting anything out of it. I'm changing that now. I bet Grace thinks I'd never make it to TV. I bet if she saw that I survived a plane crash, she wouldn't even be proud, she would just feel bad for me or something. Well Grace, I just survived a plane crash. They gave me a book deal and put me live on the air.

I hate that look she would do whenever I told her about something bad. She thought I was pathetic. There are worse people than me, I'm not even a bad person. There are sickos out there, people who kill dogs and kids. I saw a whole special on TV about people who beat animals. I'm pathetic, but I'm not sick in the head. If I wasn't in so much debt, this would be different. I'm the only person in the world who's made a bad investment? Dad says it takes money to make money. I take some money to make some money, and suddenly no one can speak to me anymore? He's always been an asshole. Always. Mom, if you're hearing this, it's not about you, okay. Mom's not going to be listening to this. Well, whatever. I'm not going to kill myself today. Or tomorrow. So if you're listening to this and I'm dead, it's probably because that creep from the bar killed me or I didn't survive a plane crash. Best of luck with everything else you do in life. Ignore me. Merry Christmas.

[PHONE CLICKS. TAPE CLICKS.]

30.
6:17 P.M., MONDAY, FEBRUARY 12, 1990

MACHINE: One new message from Monday, February 12, 6:17 P.M.

[TAPE CLICKS]

BRANDY: Peter, your machine tricked me! I'd planned to say hello in French—bonjour, if you didn't know—so when you said, "Hello?" I said, "Bonjour!" But then the machine kept going, and I realized I'd been hoodwinked. I just learned that word. Oh, listen to me, going on and on and you don't even know who this is yet. You just think I'm some French woman. Well, I'm not. I got your number through TelePersonals. You're my first match, and I'm a little nervous. I'm sorry if you can tell, which you can't, because my voice actually hides my nerves quite well. Anyway…

[PAPER SHUFFLES]

BRANDY: I'm 31 years old—only for two more days, though! Yes, I got cursed with a Valentine's birthday. You're probably thinking, "A curse?! So much chocolate in one day!" Well, I'm sick of having my chocolate intake crammed into one day. Okay, back to business.

[PAPER SHUFFLES]

BRANDY: My favorite movie is Jaws, but only because I was in it. I mean, just as an extra in a beach scene. Very lucky timing, sort of an accident, a right-place-right time kind of thing. You won't believe this, but we actually smoked a little weed while they shot the scene! You can't see that in any of the shots. You can barely see me. Blink and you miss it. I'm sorry if I put you off by talking about drugs. I was 17, although today I am for full legalization. I don't mean to get political, I just figured since it came up I'd let you know. Let's see, where are those prompts, hmm...

[PAPER SHUFFLES]

BRANDY: Um, I've read the Bible all the way through. I think my favorite verse, or at least the verse I think about the most, is Song of Solomon 2:5. It says, "Strengthen me with raisins, refresh me with apples, for I am faint with love." That's in the NIV, but then, in the King James Version, it says, "Stay me with flagons, comfort me with apples: for I am sick of love." I like thinking about how two versions of the same verse have opposite feelings about love. I thought that was interesting. Reading the whole thing was more of a curiosity than a moral obligation, if you were wondering. Which you probably weren't, your profile said you were agnostic. Which is okay with me. Anyway... let's see... My father was a plumber and my mother was a lotto-winner. It sounds tacky to describe her like that, but she believed luck is earned. She used to tell me her job was being a winner. I don't know about that, but she paid for me to go to a good school so I kept my mouth shut. I like red wine, Chinese food, and I like to watch Jeopardy.

[EXHALE. PEN TAPPING ON PAPER.]

BRANDY: Sorry I keep pausing. I tried so hard to memorize my answers that I can barely remember the questions. Oh! My favorite memory was when I was very little. Mom woke me up to watch the sunrise on the beach, and when she put me down, the sand was so cold on my bare feet. I loved the way it felt.

[PAUSE]

Isn't it weird that you can think about a feeling and, like, actually feel it in your mind? Picture your cat—your profile said you have a cat. I love cats, but I guess you assumed that since we got matched up and you put it in your deal-breakers. My only deal-breaker is good dental hygiene. I hate bad breath. I'm sorry. I know you must have good breath because you put that you have good dental hygiene. Unless you're lying. I mean, everybody lies. I don't mind people that lie sometimes. But it better not be about bad breath! I can just picture the smell of it. Where was I… that's right, your cat. Now think about touching his fur. You can feel it, right? Like, you can feel in your mind the way his fur feels under your fingers. That's amazing. To me, anyway. Well, I hope your Monday is going great, your Tuesday doesn't go too late, your Wednesday is a breeze, your Thursday goes with ease and your Friday comes as fast as you please. I made that up. I don't know if I'll keep it. I guess I rambled here too much. If you're interested, call me back. I mean, you don't—I'd like it if you called me back. I wouldn't mind a birthday call. Au revoir! That's goodbye in french. Bye, Peter.

[PAPER SHUFFLES]

BRANDY: Oh, and my eyes are green.

[PHONE CLICKS. TAPE CLICKS.]

31.
7:15 P.M., THURSDAY, JULY 14, 1988

MACHINE: One new message from Thursday, July 14, 7:15 P.M.

[BEEP]

CARL: Shirley, baby, pick up the phone, Mama. I can't do this no more. I'm all cooped up at this damn motel and I want to come home. Shirley, I am sorry. I was a bad man. You're a wonderful old lady, you cook me my meals, you make our bed. I disrespected you. I'm sorry, from the bottom of my broken heart. I ain't never gonna do that again. She didn't mean nothin. Nothin! I'm at the Bellevue, it's a damn heat wave out and this room ain't got no fan. Buncha scared lookin' white boys walkin' around here thinkin I can sell 'em somethin'...

[LAUGHING]

CARL: Lord, it's hot out tonight. I got stains on my white shirt. Not the good one, the other one. You can fix that, you always had the magic with stains. Remember when Kathleen spilled wine on the shirt your Mama got me? I never seen a stain disappear so quickly!

[LAUGHING. SIGH.]

CARL: Shirley, I don't want to eat alone no more. Eatin' McDonalds every night in a damn motel room. I wanna be back with you. I want to take you out to Paulette's. I want to make things right, baby! You have to pick up the phone. I know you're mad at me. I was just drinkin' too much again, I didn't know you were going to come home, you never called me and told me. I never woulda showed up with some woman if I knew you'd be—I mean—you know what I mean, Shirley. I'm a damn fool, but we don't want to throw away 25 years. We said we wouldn't let foolishness get in the way again.

[MUFFLED NOISES]

CARL: Listen. I was at the bar after work tonight, I heard that record Johnny got us on to when he was still workin' at Stax. I don't know the name, you know I can't remember a damn thing these days. But this song spoke to me. God knew what I needed to hear. Let me sing it for you Shirley, I used to love to sing to you.

CARL [SINGING]: I'm a fool because / I took your love for granted, girl, and I almost lost / Your sweet love and your tender / your tenderness / And a few other things I've got to add to this list, listen / Your understanding when I needed it most / That special guidance, baby, and your strong, strong support / I'm so glad that fools can fall in love / 'Cause I'm a fool in love with you (Look at me, girl, look at you, girl) / I'm so glad that fools can fall in love / Look at me, girl, look at you, girl

CARL: I coulda wrote that song about you. I'm a fool but I fell in love with you and I need you. I can't be at this damn motel no more. I want to come back home. It's dinner time and I'm hungry. Please let me back home. I know you're sittin' on that ugly blue chair by the damn answerin' machine listenin' to my ass ramble on. I'm packin' up and comin' home, Shirley. I won't ever make a mistake like that again. That wasn't me. That wasn't Carl. Let me take you to Paulette's. I'm gonna go and wait for you there, we can meet there and go home together. You deserve it, Shirley. You deserve it and more. I—

[MUFFLED NOISES]

CARL: What? No, I don't. I don't do that. I'm just using the damn phone.

I hate this damn place. Shirley, I love you and I'm sorry. You know this. A week apart is too much. I can't be here no more. I need you and the dog and that ugly chair. I—

[MUFFLED NOISES]

CARL: What? I'm almost done.

This white boy needs to use the phone, so I'm gonna go now. I'll see you soon, Shirley.

CARL [SINGING]: I'm so glad that fools can fall in love

[PHONE CLICKS. TAPE CLICKS.]

32.
11:32 A.M., MONDAY, MAY 16, 2005

VOICEMAIL: One new message from Monday, May 16, 11:32 A.M.

[BEEP]

MIGUEL: Good afternoon, Marcus, this is Miguel Serrano with the East Side Marriott shipping department. Just calling you 'cause there's two gray cases over here. They were supposed to be picked up and they're still sitting here at the shipping and receiving area. That's the, uh, the Marriott—East Side—525 Lexington, New York, New York 10017. Again, this is Miguel Serrano, calling about two cases that are over here that were supposed to be picked up, but they're still sittin' here. You're probably going to want to take care of this sooner than later. Last time we had cases that weren't picked up, I mean… And these are the gray ones. I know I said that already but I feel like I need to say it again. The phone number is 212-754-8133, extension 8247. Again, that's 212-754-8133, extension 8247. Thank you very much, have a great day. Two cases. Gray.

[PHONE CLICKS]

33.
8:03 P.M., Saturday, September 25, 1999

MACHINE: One new message from Saturday, September 25, 8:03 P.M.

[TAPE CLICKS]

NICKY: Whatsup my guy, it's Nicky. It's fuckin', 8:00 at night, I think. Dude, I gotta talk to you about this movie I just saw. Danielle is still at her movie. She went to see Runaway Bride. I'm good on that shit, you know?

Anyway, I'm at Assembly Square and just saw that fuckin' movie, The Sixth Sense? Wow. I don't know if you know about it, but wow. I gotta tell you about this. It's got John McClane as the main guy. Not like Die Hard at all, but it's fuckin' good, dude. But it's a scary movie, like, wicked scary, too.

So I don't want to give too much away, but here's the story: Bruce Willis is, like, a doctor or something, and he meets up with this little kid. Well, I guess he gets shot first. This weird creep is in his bathroom, one of his patients or whatever, and he shoots him and he—well I don't want to give too much away, but yeah, we can just say he doesn't die from the gunshot for now.

So then his wife is being a bitch, and he meets this kid who's wicked creepy, he actually looks like Patty Carson's kid? Remember that weird little fuck? So yeah, this kid tells him he sees dead people. Like he says, "I see dead people." Real creep shit, like he sees them just as normal fuckin' people. Fuckin' weird, right?

So he, like, goes around seeing all these fuckin' dead people, and doing stuff with them, and Bruce Willis is, like, with him, talking to him and shit. I don't want to say too much, but you're a fuckin' movie guy, so I bet you can see where this is going, yeah? If this kid says he sees dead people, and it's just him and Bruce hangin' out, you know? I won't say anymore, don't want to ruin the twist about him bein' a fuckin' dead guy.

Anyway, yeah, real scary shit. There was this tool a few rows in front of me who was snoring. I threw my fuckin' Kit-Kat at his head. He got fuckin' ripped, but you know he still shut the fuck up. Reminded me of when you used to fall asleep in Mr. Taglione's class. He would walk over and smack the shit out of you in front of everyone, you'd turn wicked red. Somehow you still got a better grade than me, you fuckin' prick.

Yeah, so now I'm just waiting for Danielle, whenever her movie's done. How are ya? Enjoyin' the Heights? Was just drivin' by your old place yesterday on my route, fuckin' neighborhood looks like shit, you got out at a good time. Feel bad that Bags is still over there. That fuckin guy, God bless 'em. Still walking around with that bum leg. All right dude, go see this movie, it's called The Sixth Sense. I bet you'll see that fuckin' twist comin, you're good at that shit. I was fuckin', like, "Whoa!" Fuckin' dead guy the whole time. Tell Carly I said what's up.

You going to Aunt Janet's for supper this weekend? Call me and tell me if you are. Maybe I'll see you there, your Ma was asking me if I was going and I told her I'd see what you were doing. Don't want Mr. Fuckin' Moneybags to make me look bad, though, so maybe I should keep you away. Fuckin' rich guy now, huh? Thinks he doesn't have to show his face anymore, too busy for us fuckin' delivery guys now. Come down from your ivory tower, fuckin' big shot. Mr. Cubicle-and-Paperwork guy. You still workin' out? Paperweights don't count as liftin', bro!

[LAUGHING]

NICKY: I'm just bustin' your balls, we're all proud of you. All right, gimme a call back. I'll be back home in, like, an hour. And tell me once you see this fuckin' movie, I still can't believe that fuckin' guy was dead the whole time.

[PHONE CLICKS. TAPE CLICKS.]

34.
11:35 A.M., WEDNESDAY, FEBRUARY 20, 1991

[CASSETTE TAPE CLICKS, REWINDS, CLICKS AGAIN. ANSWERING MACHINE BEEPS.]

MACHINE: One new message from Wednesday, February 20, 11:35 A.M.

[BEEP]

UNKNOWN: Hey, it's me, call me back.

[PHONE CLICKS. TAPE CLICKS.]

Photo: Diana Ericksen

AUSTIN ABBOTT is a writer and filmmaker based in New York. His writing has been featured in the Washingtonville High School newspaper (2008-2009) and his film MIKE (2020) apparently won a Critic's Choice Award at the 2019 L'AGE D'OR INTERNATIONAL ARTHOUSE FILM FESTIVAL in Kolkata, India. I TRIED CALLING is his first book.